Become a star reader with Caillou!

This three-level reading series is designed for pre-readers or beginning readers and is based on popular Caillou episodes. The books feature common sight words used with limited grammar. Each book also offers a set number of target words. These words are noted in bold print and are presented in a picture dictionary in order to reinforce meaning and expand reading vocabulary.

For pre-readers to read along

- 125-175 words
- Simple sentences
- Simple vocabulary and common sight words
- Picture dictionary teaching 6 target words

For beginning readers to read with support

- 175-250 words
- Longer sentences
- Limited vocabulary and more sight words
- Picture dictionary teaching 8 target words

For improving readers to read on their own or with support

- 250-350 words
- Longer sentences and more complex grammar
- Varied vocabulary and less-common sight words
- Picture dicti[illegible] teaching 10 target words

Text: adaptation by Rebecca Klevberg Moeller
All rights reserved.
Original story written by Sarah Margaret Johanson, based on the animated series CAILLOU
Illustrations: Eric Sévigny, based on the animated series CAILLOU

Chouette Publishing would like to thank the Government of Canada and SODEC for their financial support.

Bibliothèque et Archives nationales du Québec and Library and Archives Canada cataloguing in publication

Moeller, Rebecca Klevberg
Caillou: Getting Dressed With Daddy

(Read with Caillou. Level 1)

Previously published as: Dress-up with daddy.

For children aged 3 and up.

ISBN 978-2-89718-471-1 (softcover)

1. Caillou (Fictitious character) - Juvenile fiction. 2. Clothing and dress - Juvenile fiction. I. Pleau-Murissi, Marilyn - Dress-up with daddy. II. Title.

PS8626.O432G47 2018 jC813'.3 C2017-942126-3
PS9626.O432G47 2018

Printed in Canada

10 9 8 7 6 5 4 3 2 1 CHO2029 MAR2018

Getting Dressed with Daddy

Text: Rebecca Klevberg Moeller, Language Teaching Expert
Illustrations: Eric Sévigny, based on the animated series

Caillou wants to get dressed.
He has no clothes.

Daddy helps Caillou find some clothes.

Hmm, no clothes here.

Uh-oh, Mommy is washing
clothes!

Daddy has an idea. Caillou can wear Daddy's clothes.

What? Daddy's clothes are
big. Caillou is **little**.

Daddy finds some **shorts**.

He gives the **shorts** to Caillou.

But Caillou can't wear them.
He is too **little**.

Caillou puts on the **shorts**.
They are too **big**.

Daddy adds a **belt**. Now they are not too **big**.

Next, Daddy brings a **shirt**.

Caillou laughs. It is too **big**.

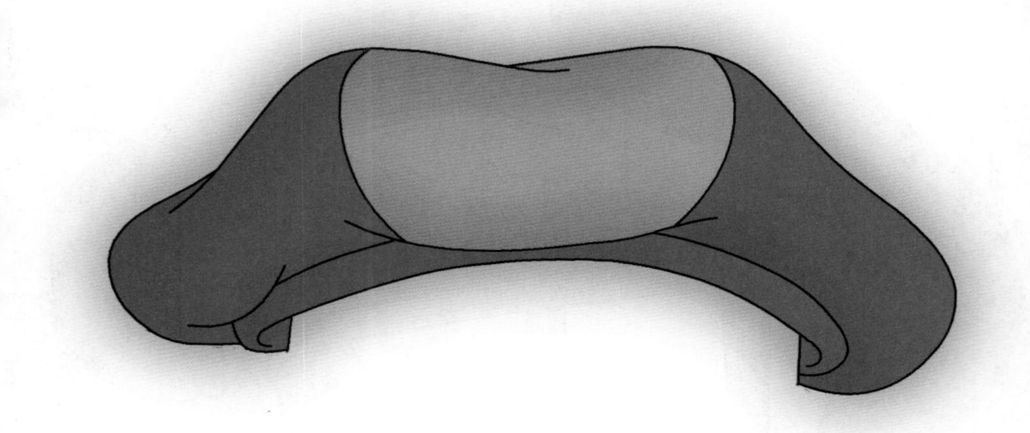

Daddy adds a **hat**.

Almost dressed.

Daddy ties Caillou's **belt**.

Mommy sees Caillou's **shorts**, **belt**, **shirt** and **hat**.

She laughs.

Caillou looks like a **big** boy.

Daddy has one more idea.
A mustache!

Caillou looks funny.
A mustache looks funny on
a little boy.

Mommy takes a picture. Smile,
big boy Caillou!

Picture Dictionary

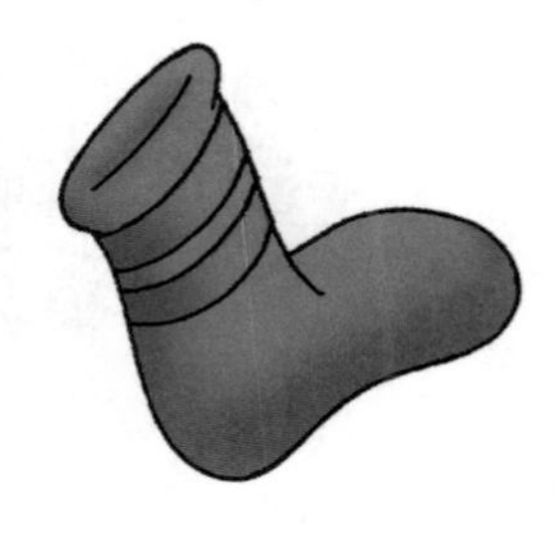

big

little

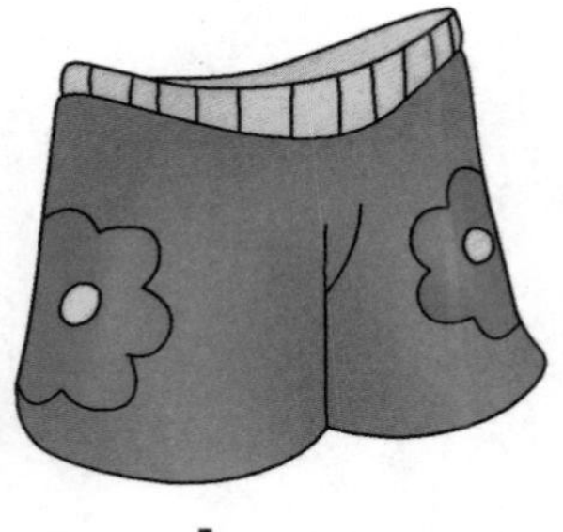

shorts

belt

shirt

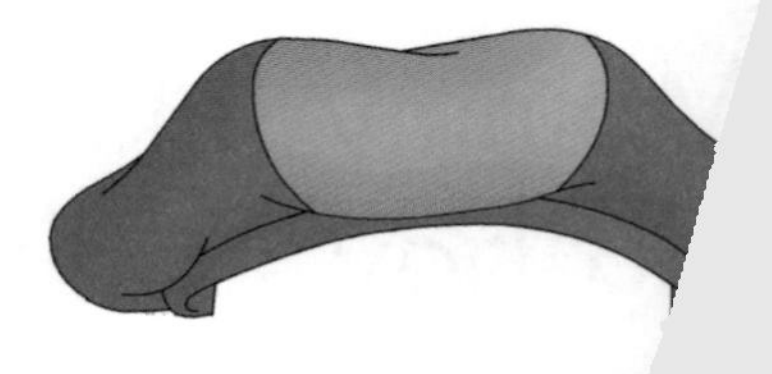

hat